Sandy Creek
NEW YORK

An Imprint of Sterling Publishing
387 Park Avenue South
New York, NY 10016

ISBN 978-1-4351-4762-1

Manufactured in China
Lot #:
2 4 6 8 10 9 7 5 3 1
06/13

To the children
in Akeman Street
R.P.

The Pirate House

Rebecca Patterson

Sandy Creek
NEW YORK

No one knew who lived in that house on the corner. But when all those seagulls flew onto the roof, Sam Turner said it must be . . .

PIRATES!

And we knew it WAS pirates when we saw the tide had gone out of their pond and there was a shell and some GOLD left in the bottom!

We never looked at the pirate laundry.

If you did you turned into a jellyfish.

Even on a sunny day we could hear the wind howling inside the pirate house.

And someone said that once a fish
fell out of the mail slot.

The mailman had to mail it back.

Turner says that at night sea fills the house and it OWS like an aquarium.

But the pirates never come out. They are busy having parties for baby mermaids . . .

...and counting their gold.

Last Thursday, the front door of the pirate house started to open . . .

Sam Turner shouted, "HOLD YOUR BREATH! A HUGE WAVE WILL COME OUT!"

So we all held our breath.

The door opened wider . . . and wider . . .

But it wasn't a wave that came out.
Or a pirate. It was . . .

. . . a **LADY**, and she told us
to stop leaning on her fence.

We said to Sam Turner, "That's NOT a pirate!"
And we all went home for our dinner.

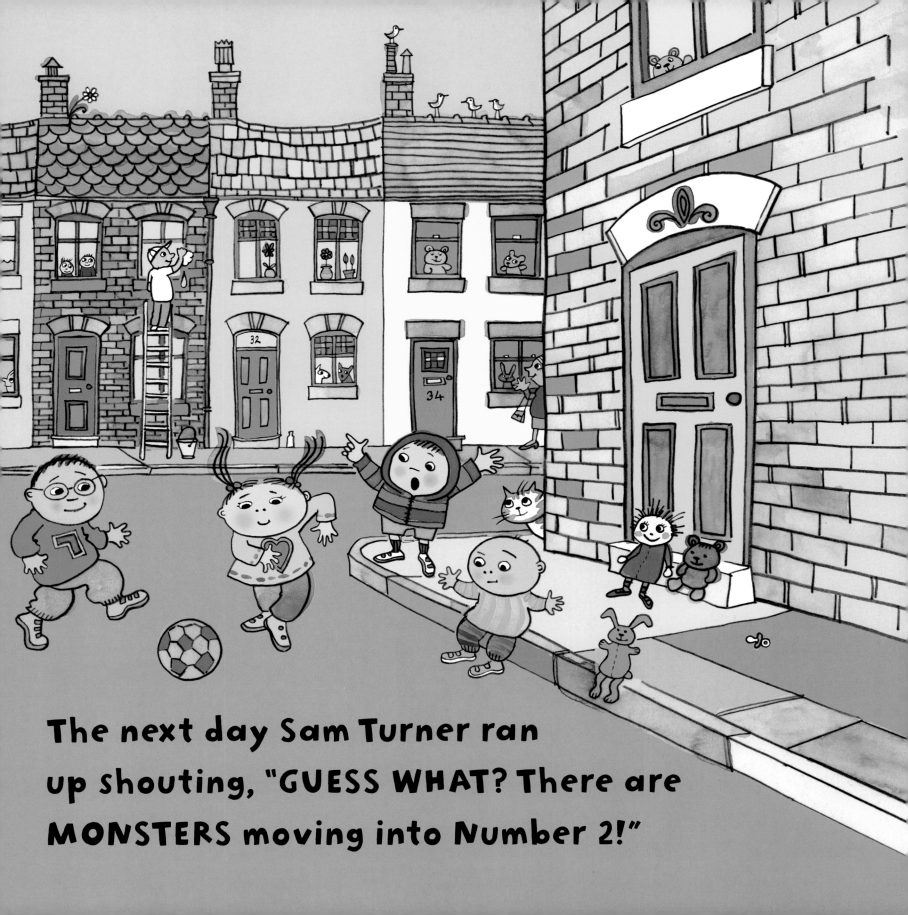

The next day Sam Turner ran up shouting, "GUESS WHAT? There are MONSTERS moving into Number 2!"

We laughed and said to Sam Turner,

"Sam, there are **NO** monsters moving into Number 2, and there are **NO** pirates in that house on the corner, because . . .